The Unbelievable BUBBLE Book

The Unbelievable BUBBLE Book

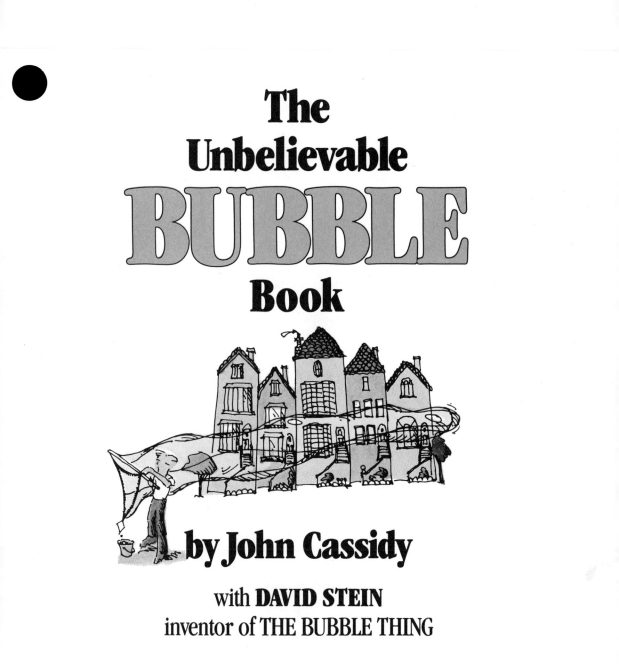

by John Cassidy

with **DAVID STEIN**
inventor of THE BUBBLE THING

KLUTZ®

KLUTZ® is an independent publishing company staffed entirely by real human beings. We began our corporate life back in 1977 in a Palo Alto, California garage that we shared with a Chevrolet Impala. Back then, founders John Cassidy, Darrell Hack and BC Rimbeaux were all students and one of the founding principles was thusly stated: be in and out of business by the end of summer vacation.

So much for that plan.

Plan B? Create the best-written, best-looking, most imaginative books in the world. Be honest and fair in all our dealings. Work hard to make every day feel like the first day of summer vacation.

We aim high.

We'd love to hear your comments about this book.

Write us.

KLUTZ®

455 Portage Avenue
Palo Alto, CA 94306

Additional Copies:

Give us a call at (650) 857-0888 and we'll help track down your nearest Klutz retailer. Should they be out of stock, additional copies of this book as well as the entire library of 100% Klutz certified books, are available in the Klutz Catalogue.
See the last page
for details.

To Glinda.

What's This Thing Attached to the Book?

BUBBLE-WISE, the American consumer has been getting short changed for years. The bubbles that come out of a dime store bottle of soap solution are not really bubbles, they're micro-bubbles, pygmies of the race.

And you're about to see why.

The odd-looking apparatus attached to the front of this book is the patented creation of David Stein, an inventor from Montana. It consists of a two-piece plastic rod designed to suspend a fringe loop that slides along the tube like a curtain. A simple enough design—until you see what it can do.

David Stein's Bubble Thing makes bubbles bigger than modern science used to think possible. Mountain bubbles. Block busting bubbles. Bubbles the size of cars before the gas crisis.

Three things make David Stein bubbles possible.

1. The open-and-close-ability of the loop

Slide the bubble loop closed and it becomes dunkable in a small bucket of suds. Then open, wave, and close again to control the size and shape of your emerging bubble.

2. The nature of the fabric

The small capillaries in the fabric soak up lots of soap. The large pores hold more for quick release. Its flatness lets the fabric close neatly, and its roughness helps the bubble film attach.

3. Humidity

Bubbles love humidity. Bubble film is so thin that very dry air causes it to evaporate quickly.

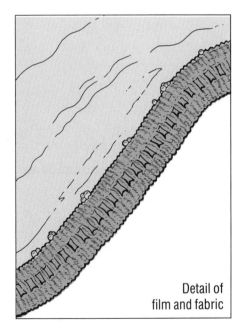

Detail of
film and fabric

Hundreds of different things were tried before settling on the kind of fabric you see here. Everything from chain to yarn. Nothing performs as well as the ladder-weave fabric used on this updated model of the Bubble Thing.

Good Bubble Conditions

BUBBLES LOVE high humidity. They prefer cool, shady areas, sheltered from the wind. The finest bubble days are foggy or overcast. Best of all, try right after a rain. No matter what the weather, you can usually find pools of air damp, cool, or quiet enough to make impressive bubbles.

On dry days, look for higher humidity near trees or water. Trees, bushes, grass, anything with green leaves transpires water vapor into the air. (They also remove carbon dioxide, which is poison to bubbles.)

On hot days, cool your bubbles in the shade. Tall buildings work as well as trees. Just moving into a building shadow makes an enormous difference. Also try in the early morning when air is cool and calm (and colors especially beautiful!). Don't miss the cool evening, my favorite time.

Wind can be a problem to something as fragile as bubbles. Look out the window when you get the bubble urge. If the trees are quiet, you're in luck. Even if they're rustling, you'll still find quiet pools of air behind buildings or in the woods. And every neighborhood has a courtyard, cul-de-sac, or two where air is magically still, even in a gusty breeze. On a windy beach, try behind the dunes.

Bubbles rise on updrafts. Try courtyards, tall building alleyways, small valleys, and slopes of hills.

Of all the factors which affect bubbles, most people find humidity the most puzzling. Humidity is invisible (except as fog). In the early days of the Bubble Thing, the same soap would give wonderful bubbles one day, and disappointing ones the next, leaving everyone mystified. The humidity had simply changed. Then one day, a humidity gauge was obtained (ask at your hardware store) and the mystery was solved.

BUBBLE PEOPLE

DAVID STEIN. World famous for inventing the Bubble Thing, currently marketed from Iceland to Kuala Lumpur, David Stein is "an unreformed Montana ranch kid," meaning he survived Harvard and can still dig a ditch with satisfaction. Since about 1955, he has worked as a gravity irrigator, hayhand, soda jerk, surveyor, designer/builder, candlemaker, college professor, unspecialized communard, snail gatherer, salmon fisherman, Montessori teacher, Zen student, architect, landscape architect, and international bubble magnate. "It looks terrible on your manuscript." He is happily married, has a bright little daughter, who inspired Bubble Thing, three large fun-loving step-kids and motley animals. He wants to thank Mom, Dad, Katherine, David, Joey, Raphael, Rebecca, Murphy, Lisa and Jennifer. His ambition is to blow a 30-foot sphere.

David Stein in action

Bubbles and Humidity

B UBBLE·THING sized bubbles need high humidity conditions to really perform. You can't ski without snow, you can't sail without wind, and you can't amaze your neighbors with 8-foot bubble blimps on a very dry day. But even the driest days work fine for the 1-2 footers.

Dry, 50% humidity.

Early mornings are usually good, even on dry days. This was taken at 10 a.m. when the humidity was still 65%. Later that afternoon it would drop to 35%

Bubble Heaven. 90% humidity

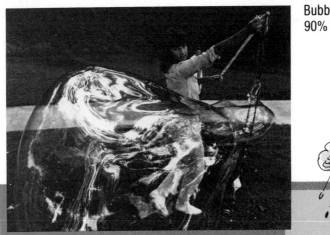

Putting Your Bubble Thing Together

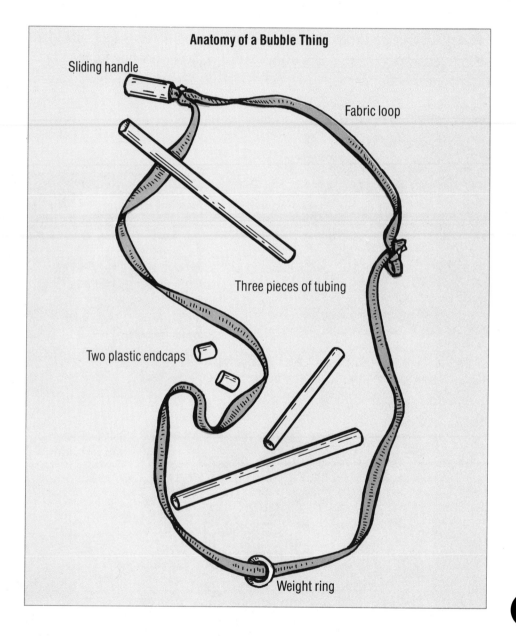

Anatomy of a Bubble Thing

Sliding handle

Fabric loop

Three pieces of tubing

Two plastic endcaps

Weight ring

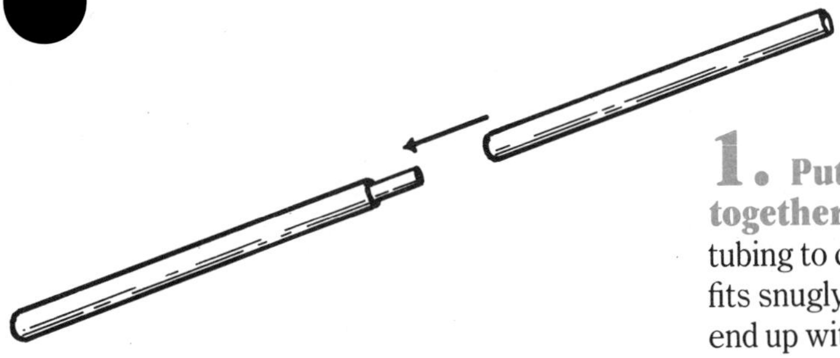

1. **Putting the plastic tube together.** Use the short slit piece of tubing to connect the other two. It fits snugly inside them. You should end up with one 22 inch tube.

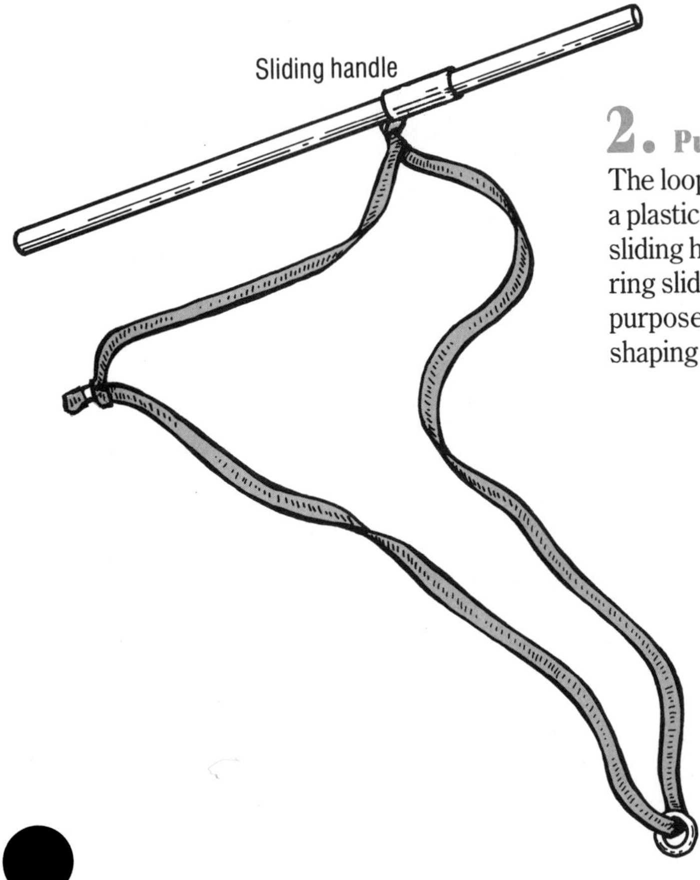

Sliding handle

2. **Putting the fabric loop on.** The loop has a sliding handle and a plastic ring attached to it. Slip the sliding handle over the tube. Let the ring slide freely along the loop. Its purpose is to give better control in shaping the bubbles.

Weight ring

3. The fabric loop also has a knot in it which you should tuck into one end of the tube and then cover with an endcap. In doing this, make sure the fabric is not twisted. Most critical, make sure the two strands of fabric overlap at the endcap.

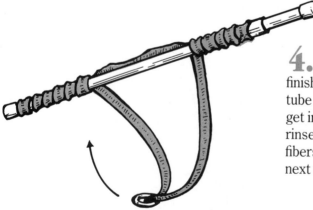

4. Wrapping up. When you're finished, whirl the fringe around the tube so it doesn't drag and generally get in the way. And don't forget to rinse out the congealed soap so the fibers are clean and open for the next time.

Cooking Up the Bubble Mixture:
or, The Joy of Bubbles

AFTER A GREAT DEAL of grocery store research, I have been forced to concede an inalienable fact: Procter & Gamble's Joy, *clear* Ivory or *green* Dawn liquid detergents are the way to go. My own preference is for Joy or *clear* Ivory, but there exists a vocal school of bubble makers who swear by *green* Dawn. (*Blue* Dawn used to work, but Procter & Gamble changed the formula.) Maybe local water conditions make the difference.

I should mention that this is an unbiased review of the detergent world. Much as I would like, I receive no commission on detergent sales. With that disclaimer out of the way, herewith follows my Basic Bubbles recipe which is good for normal weather conditions. For very dry days, add 10%–50% more water.

BASIC BUBBLES

1 clean pail
1 cup Joy, *clear* Ivory or *green* Dawn
3–4 tablespoons glycerine (optional, from your pharmacy)
12 cups clean, cold water (up to 50% more on dry days)

Directions

1. Measure 12 cups water into the pail. Add 1 cup dish soap.

2. Add the glycerine. In most atmospheres, it makes the bubbles more durable by reducing evaporation.

3. Stir, but not too much. You don't want froth on the top because it tends to break the bubbles. If you get any, skim it off with your hand.

Big League Bubble Building

YOU'VE PUT the Bubble Thing together, mixed up your solution, and found the right air. If this is going to be your neighborhood's first exposure to unbelievable bubbles, you should be aware that you are about to become a smallish tourist attraction and traffic hazard. Use some discretion and don't try to float massive bubbles in front of unsuspecting motorists. Keep the soap out of your eyes, and if you have any spills, clean them up before you go.

Soap is slippery. Avoid smooth marble pavements and especially metal gratings. Stay on rough, non-skid surfaces: earth, concrete, asphalt, grass. Clean up any spills before you go.

Don't let little kids scamper under the loop. Don't swing carelessly. Avoid suds in your eyes (stings slightly), or too much on your hands (rinse).

Pick up the Bubble Thing. Hold the tube in your left hand, and the sliding handle in your right. Slide the loop open and closed a few times until it seems easy.

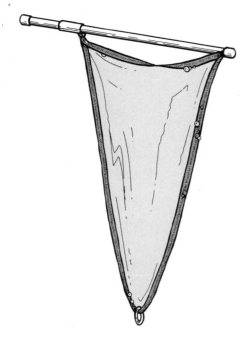

Raise the loop, still closed, vertically and pause above the bucket to let the excess soap drain back in.

Slide the loop open a little and look for a film of soap between the two strands of fabric. If nothing is there, you didn't dip all the way in, or you just need some warm-up time. Dip and raise the loop again.

When you can create a film by sliding the loop open, you're ready to go. The basic big bubble is created just by moving the loop sideways through the air. Open . . . hold open . . . and close. See the illustration. Try for a big round shape, not a long, skinny hot dog, which will collapse and burst.

Once you learn to complete your bubbles by sliding the loop closed, you'll be able to make a half-dozen large bubbles, or several dozen smaller ones on a single dunking.

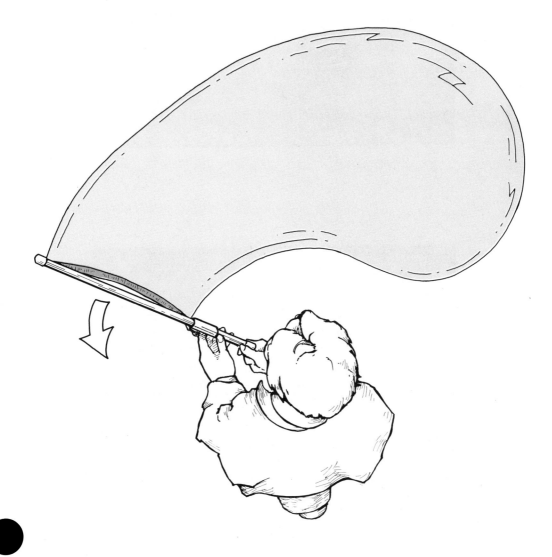

17

The Basic Big Bubble...

1. Let the excess drip into the bucket.

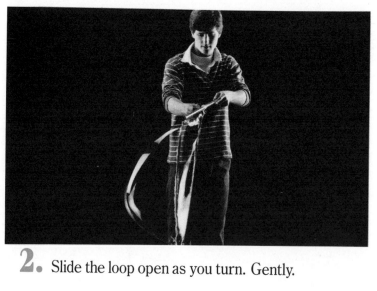

2. Slide the loop open as you turn. Gently.

3. Close the loop just as gently.

4. Finis.

Trouble-Shooting

PROBLEM
I dip the loop in the bucket, but when I spread the loop, no film.

SUGGESTION
Make sure the two strands of fabric overlap at the endcap. Then dip again. Dip the *entire* loop.

PROBLEM
Still no soap film.

SUGGESTION
Did you use Joy, *clear* Ivory or *green* Dawn? Other soaps really will not perform. Did you measure accurately? With a cup?

PROBLEM
Now I'm using one of those soaps, and still no soap film.

SUGGESTIONS
Are you standing in a high wind? Go behind a building or someplace out of the wind.

PROBLEM
Okay, now I'm standing in a dead calm, and still no film.

SUGGESTIONS
You must be standing in very dry air. Go someplace cooler, hopefully overcast, a little foggy even. Find some humidity. Near trees or water. In the shade. Try at night. Try right after a rain. And review the Good Bubble Conditions material on pages 4 and 5.

P ROBLEM
Bubbles keep popping in my face.

S UGGESTION
Turn around to put the wind at your back.

P ROBLEM
The breeze is getting worse. They're popping.

S UGGESTIONS
Make smaller bubbles. Save the big ones for moments of calm between the gusts.

PROBLEM

Your fringe loop has gotten tangled up because you've been ignoring me and sticking the end of the tube in the bucket and stirring it around.

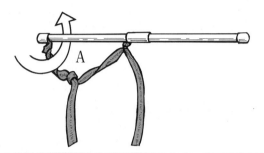

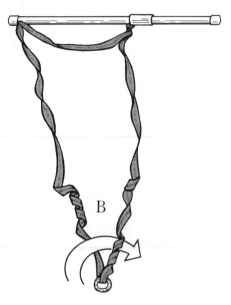

If the loop is twisted at the top, rotate the end of the tube through the space marked "A". One way will worsen the tangle and the other will fix it.

If the loop is twisted at the bottom, flip the hanging blue ring through space "B". Again, one way will worsen the tangle and the other will fix it.

PROBLEM

I'm about half-way through the bucket, and bubbles are starting to pop all the time.

SUGGESTIONS

Froth (which tends to pop big bubbles) may be building up on the loop and on top of the solution. Close the loop, and run it through your fingers, squeezing out all the froth. Also use your hand to skim froth off the top of the solution. It may also help to stir the solution just a little.

PROBLEM
A crowd of little kids keep popping the bubbles.

SUGGESTIONS
Organize them: "Okay, everybody take 3 giant steps backwards." Repeat as necessary.

Or give them guidelines: "Only pop the little bubbles, and I'll tell you which those are."

If they ignore you, try blowing a few small bubbles over their heads. While they're occupied with those, you can try for a big one.

PROBLEM
The loop is too long for little kids to use. It drags on the ground.

SUGGESTIONS
Shorten the loop by stuffing some of it into the endcap. Make sure the two strands overlap when you recap.

PROBLEM
We stopped for a while, and now the loop isn't working very well.

SUGGESTIONS
The fabric fibers are plugged by congealed soap. Rinse thoroughly, and you're ready to go again.

Advanced Bubble Thing

BY DAVID STEIN

Okay, let's assume you're happily through the trouble stage, you've wiped off your hands and are ready to read further. Fool around enough and you'll discover most of what follows yourself. These are just hints.

Bubble Thing is a smooth, gentle sort of motion. Don't be jerky. Open . . . close. If there's no wind, swing slowly sideways. Or just walk.

Most people get long tubes first, because they forget to close the loop. Tubes are fun and spectacular, but they don't last long. If you try to close one off and set it free, it will collapse end to end like a rubber band and pop. Sometimes the break starts at one end, and just goes rrrrr . . . . ip. All the way.

Big spheres take calm air and timing. Slide the loop wide open at first to get the bubble started as fat as possible. Don't stretch the fabric though, which causes popping. Hold open long enough (split seconds count here!) to form a fat blimpy oblong. Then round off and separate. The blimp will contract end to end, forming a sphere.

When making big ones, keep an eye on the center of the upper loop. A thick river of soap flowing from there means you have the juice for a big bubble. Learn to size your bubbles by watching that flow.

In humid weather, you'll get 5 or 6 big ones per dip. Maybe 20 to 30 smaller models.

Tubes and spheres. Those are just convenient words from geometry class. A bubble is really a spherical wave, a big one undulates slowly like the ocean, flows with the air, almost alive. A so-called sphere will suddenly become a whale leaping straight up, then dive, or flatten out and come at you like a manta ray. Or go snaking round the corner, or creep slowly up the roof, then spurt away in the breeze over the roof ridge.

After a while, Bubble Thing will make you sensitive to the air. You'll respond to the slightest motion, like fishes do in water. It's a nice feeling. You'll learn the secret invisible movements of air through your neighborhood; you'll find updrafts. In my own neighborhood, there's a tall C-shaped courtyard, where no bubble can escape. Instead, it will spiral up 8, 10, 12 stories. There's another spot where the river breeze splashes up the facade of a building. The bubbles either zoom up the wall or whirl around the corner, scaring unsuspecting pedestrians. Some days, on that same corner, there's a great "ferris wheel" of air, that carries the bubbles way up 6 or 8 stories, down the other corner, and round and round in a perfect wheel.

And then, two blocks away, there's a 30-story building where the bubbles go updrafting straight up the lee side, grazing window after window till they reach the top and sail away in the wind. I also know a sidewalk grating with warm air always rising, but that's cheating.

26

People bubbling on city rooftops are often surprised to find that bubbles fall. Friends have spent many happy lunch hours dropping bubble spheres on pedestrians below.

Some updrafts result from thermals. I gridlocked Provincetown one night, by launching wave after wave of 6-footers ascending stepwise up into the fog like some kind of angel staircase. Later I learned the whole Cape Cod peninsula (and other beach areas as well) create rising thermals, because sand retains the sun's warmth.

No skyscrapers or thermals? Stand just downwind of the house. The air often curls upwards there and will carry your bubbles up the roof. Or stand just downwind of a large ball-shaped tree. Air flowing under foliage may lift your bubbles into the windshadow above.

Quiet air? Look for motionless tree leaves. Even in a breeze, there's often one tree standing in a calm eddy.

Bubbles bounce on water if the surface is calm. They'll bounce way out across a pond, kissing their own reflections each time. Sometimes one will settle, form a dome—long lasting too because of the high humidity. If a dome is big enough, try swimming under, and stick your head up in there. And try bubbles over surf.

If you use Bubble Thing indoors, you're responsible for the furniture. Stay off the slick floors. Put a sheet or some towels under the bucket to protect the carpet.

In calm air, try the following special tricks.

Jonah-in-a-Bubble

Make a 6 incher, then enclose it in a larger one. The little bubble will bounce around inside.

Doughnut

Just open the loop halfway, and spin around. Takes timing. To my knowledge, no one has ever connected the ends.

Pendulum

Hold the loop six inches open, swing it in a tight circle. Baby bubbles will peel off.

Double Bubble

Make one bubble. Then hook on a second. Repeat for clusters and chains.

That's about it. You have reached the frontier of bubblemaking in the 20th century. From here on, experiment!

David Stein

Homemade Bubble Machines

Here are some do-it-yourself bubble makers that you can build with nothing but household odds and ends. They make pretty big bubbles, so if you use them indoors you'd better have a mop handy. For best results, as usual, use the Basic Bubbles recipe.

Two Straws and a String

Bernie Zubrowski of the Boston Children's Museum was one of the first to popularize this simple little collapsible bubble loop. It appears in his excellent book "Bubbles."

Tie a piece of string through two straws and then dip into a cookie sheet of bubble solution. Carefully lift it up and pull it back towards you.

The trick is in flipping the frame up or down to break off a bubble. (Practice.)

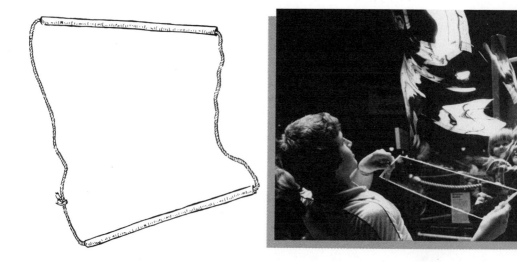

Frying Pan and Coathanger

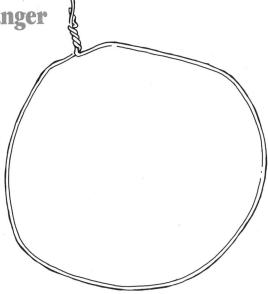

Bending a coathanger into a loop without a little kink at the top is actually pretty tricky, probably requiring the services of a pair of pliers. But once you've managed that, you can fill a frying pan with Basic Bubbles and create some pretty impressive spheres. Wave your loop gently through the air and rotate it to complete a bubble.

Plastic Six Pack Holder

Bubbles to go. Just dip this into the solution and wave it around. Bubble clusters galore.

Tin Can Horn

Cut both the tops and bottoms out of a couple of similar size cans and tape the two of them together. Put a window of film on the end of one of them and hold at arm's length when you blow through (this helps to make the airflow smoother and not as prone to break the film).

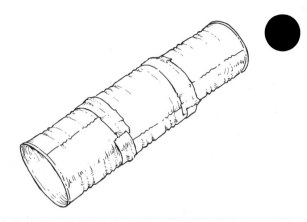

Two Hands

The ultimate in unencumbered bubble making. As usual, you can use Basic Bubbles for your solution (although Sterling Johnson, a bare-handed bubble master, recommends Ivory liquid). The trick is to blow a steady, controlled stream of air. As in the case of tin can bubbles, do it at arm's length for a steadier air stream.

To release the bubble from your hands, you have to seal the opening off. Gently slide your hands over one another until the opening between them is gone, then finish by bringing them together, palm to palm. It's tricky, but impressive.

Sterling Johnson, a San Francisco attorney and bare-handed bubble specialist, demonstrates the technique.

Cookie Sheet Bubbles

You can build entire dome bubble landscapes on a cookie sheet with a straw and a little bit of breath control. Start with enough solution to fill a cookie sheet about ¼" deep. Dip your straw into the solution and pull it out. This creates a small "window" of bubble film on the end of the straw. Then, holding the tip of the straw just above the surface of your bubble solution, blow a small bubble onto the solution. Carefully inflate it to a full-size dome, then lift the straw out of the bubble (gently) and repeat.

If you use a couple of tin cans taped together, you can make much bigger bubble domes, but it takes a little more finesse to remove the tin can from the bubble without bursting it.

Sculpting Bubbles

David Stein bubbles may be the crowd-stoppers, but small-scale bubble sculptures are, in their own way, equally amazing. For tools, all you need is bubble solution (homemade is better), a soda straw, and your average kitchen. A dime store wand can be useful too, the kind that comes in the bottle of soap solution.

Tom Noddy demonstrates one of his bubble creations, the smoke-filled pentagonal prism.

The Bubble Inside a Bubble (Easy Style and Tricky)

Easy Style.

Create a small, apple sized bubble. You can use a dime store wand, a couple of tin cans with the tops and bottoms cut out... anything appropriate.

Catch the bubble on the wetted lip of a glass, or back on the wand. Now, with a soda straw already dipped into solution, poke into the larger bubble and inflate a smaller one (or two!). Dislodging the small bubble from the end of the straw takes just a little twist.

You can also put bubble domes inside one another with the same technique. Just use the straw in a thin layer of solution on the bottom of a cookie sheet to blow the first big bubble, then reach into it to inflate the inside bubble domes.

Tricky Style

Start with a smallish (apple-sized) bubble caught on a wand, a cup or something similar. Then use an extremely polite little cough, focused from about 6 inches away, aimed at a small point on the bubble's wall. The idea is to blow a small bubble into the bigger bubble, without breaking either, and without dislodging the larger bubble from its perch. This takes breath control and no amount of instructions are a substitute for a little practice. You're a budding bubble master when you can do this.

Caterpillars

Start with a smallish bubble that you've caught back on your wand or on the end of your tin can bubble tube. Using a straw dipped in solution and lifted back out, blow another bubble onto the bottom of the first, in a chain. Hold the can up so that the chain is hanging down. With a little luck and breath control, you should be able to add as many as half-a-dozen bubbles this way.

The Square Bubble

The easiest place to do this trick is on a cookie sheet with a thin layer of solution on the bottom. Blow a cluster of four equal sized bubbles together. Then reach into the cluster with a soapy wet straw and blow a fifth bubble that separates the other four. The fifth will be shaped like a square with a dome top.

It is possible to do this trick with a cluster of bubbles hanging off a tin can tube, but you'd have to start with a cluster of 6 same-size bubbles clumped together, and then reach inside with a straw to blow the inside, 7th bubble. Trickier.

Another variation on this theme is to start with a wire frame shaped like a cube. You can make such a frame with paper clips and soda straws. Cut the straws in half and connect them at the corners with paper clips that you have bent apart.

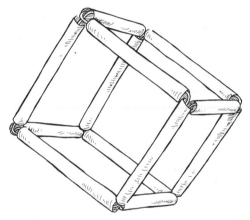

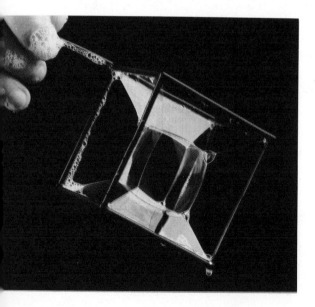

Now dip this whole apparatus into a pail of soap solution and pull it out. Notice the arrangement of bubble film. You can push your straw into the center of this and inflate a bubble which will then be constricted by the bubble film already there. Depending on where you locate the inside bubble, you can make a variety of complex geometrical shapes. All of which, incidentally, are mathematically predictable based on recent research and the "law of least effort" (see pages 61 and 62).

THE EXPLORATORIUM BUBBLE FESTIVALS

THE EXPLORATORIUM is San Francisco's famed hands-on science museum and amazement center. Founded in 1969 by Frank Oppenheimer, the Exploratorium has sponsored many special events, but none have had the mass appeal of its two bubble festivals.

The first was held in April 1984 and drew such a response that The World's Second Bubble Festival was held April 1986. Both events drew national media attention and standing room only crowds to its exhibits and demonstrations. Many science museums across the country now maintain permanent bubble exhibits, and several have also sponsored bubble festivals.

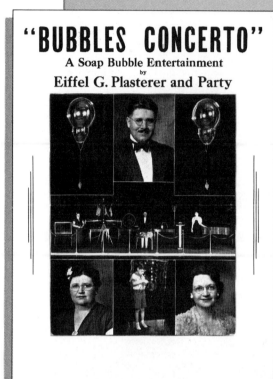

"BUBBLES CONCERTO"
A Soap Bubble Entertainment
by
Eiffel G. Plasterer and Party

EIFFEL PLASTERER is a retired high school physics teacher who lives on a farm near Huntington, Indiana. He raises sorghum, brews his own brand of anti-arthritis molasses, collects old steam engines and claims to be "the craziest man you will ever see."

For proof, Mr. Plasterer will lead you to his barn. There, Eiffel Plasterer, the mild-mannered 82 year old farmer with the friendly white goatee turns into . . . the one and only . . . "Professor Bubbles, creator of the world famous Bubble Concerto."

Just like its creator, the Bubble Concerto is a one-of-a-kind, a combination of science, soapsuds and show business, starring Eiffel Plasterer and his amazing mastery of the ordinary soap bubble.

Mr. Plasterer is the Beethoven of soap bubbles. He builds four foot bubble chains, multi-colored bubble castles, hydrogen bubbles that explode into mid-air puffs of flame. He can put bubbles inside of bubbles, or ships inside of bubbles. He can even put *you* inside of a bubble, if you care to step forward.

He is also the owner of a geriatric bubble, a 340 day old specimen preserved inside a bell jar on the shelf of his barn-cum-bubble-laboratory. "The really old ones are like soldiers," Eiffel explains, "they don't die, they just eventually fade away."

Eiffel Plasterer has performed his Bubble Concerto 1,400 times over more than 50 years, in venues ranging from the Huntington Rotary Club to the Dick Cavett show. He's even performed what has to be the world's only radio bubble show.

These days Eiffel is not out on the road quite so much, although he still manages to get in 20 or so shows a year, assisted by his daughter. He traveled in 1986 to San Francisco's Exploratorium Bubble Festival, where his show was standing room only and where he was able to talk shop with most of the other serious soap bubble practitioners—a small but dedicated fraternity for whom Eiffel Plasterer is the elder statesman, resident wizard and spiritual grandfather.

The Bubble Concerto in 1940 . . .

. . . and in 1986

BUBBLE PEOPLE

TOM NODDY. If Eiffel Plasterer is a bubble world hall of famer, Tom Noddy, who first began performing with bubbles 17 years ago, is one of its current stars.

Tom Noddy works almost exclusively with a dime store jar of bubble solution and a little plastic wand. Armed with this rather unspectacular set of props, Noddy has made dozens of national TV appearances and is practically a regular on the Johnny Carson Show. Put very briefly, Tom Noddy can do things with bubbles that should be impossible. He sculpts them into: cubes, tetrahedrons, dodecahedrons, triangular prisms, carousels, caterpillars, and bubbles inside of bubbles inside of bubbles. He creates smoke filled bubbles, "nuclear" bubbles ("perfectly safe") and bubble animals.

His secret? He's a breath control virtuoso, a talent developed originally while preparing for a hitch-hiking tour of Europe. ("I brought along about 10 bottles of soap solution.")

He would stop from time to time and, with his growing bag of bubble tricks, draw a crowd of amazed onlookers. By the time he got back, he was a regular bubble troubadour.

In the U.S., Noddy still travels a great deal, demonstrating his unique artform wherever he goes, receiving, he says, "... the same rapt attention at a logger's bar on the Olympic peninsula as at a children's center. The fascination is universal. It touches the child in each of us."

Soap Bubble Science

 BOUT 20 YEARS AGO, Raquel Welch appeared in a memorable science fiction epic in which she and her cohorts were shrunk to the size of microbes. Raquel and her team then spent a lot of time battling through the innards of a famous scientist with a health problem. Boating through his arteries, wrestling renegade corpuscles and nasty-looking germs. Great movie.

In the course of my research for this book, though, I have discovered something startling about this film: *It's not possible!*

The reason, it turns out, has to do with the very same phenomenon that enables bubbles to form: surface tension.

To illustrate. Let's say you've just stumbled through a wrong door and been miniaturized to the size of a gnat who can't swim. Then someone drops you onto a puddle of water. It could be a tough series of breaks.

But what happens?

If you're lucky, you won't even get wet. You'll bounce around on top. To someone your size, a puddle is nothing but an over-filled water bed.

If you're not lucky, if there's enough force to your fall to get you through the surface, you'll find yourself in the interesting position of being *inside* a body of water that seems to be covered with some kind of hide.

Precisely the same predicament that would have confronted Ms. Welch and her microbe-sized friends with the first drop of liquid they encountered.

The problem is water's peculiar affection for itself. It clumps together, forming a "skin" that to someone the size of a miniature Raquel Welch might well prove a daunting obstacle.

The reason, of course, is water's surface tension, a simple phenomenon with some unsimple reasons for being.

Water Skin

The easiest way to visualize surface tension is to imagine that any body of water, from the Mediterranean Sea to a thimbleful, is covered by a thin elastic skin. You can see this skin most clearly in a dripping faucet. Each drop hangs from the faucet, suspended by its "skin," until its own weight becomes too much, and it falls. (Don't take this vision too seriously though. You can't peel off water skin like an orange. Water surface *behaves* in some ways like a skin. But it is not really a skin.)

The question becomes, why is the surface of the water any different from the bulk of it?

The answer to this, unfortunately, gets down to the molecular level, the real nitty-gritty.

Water molecules are probably unlike most molecules you're familiar with. Most molecules are electrically balanced, but the three atoms that make up a water molecule are oriented in such a way that one end of the molecule has a slight positive charge, and one end, a slight negative charge. As a result, a water molecule is electrically uneven.

Since electrical opposites attract, the result of this charge imbalance is that water molecules nest together rather affectionately, one molecule's negative end held by another molecule's positive end.

Imagine a swimming pool full of these clutching molecules. Inside the swimming pool, the molecules are oriented randomly since each molecule is surrounded on all sides by other molecules and thus finds itself pulled in all directions equally.

But on the surface of the pool, things are different. Those molecules on the surface of the pool are being pulled in all directions *except up*, because there's nothing above them but air. If you want to move one of these surface molecules up and away from its grabby neighbors, you're going to have to do some work. And it's the need to do this work that creates surface tension.

If you would like to experience some of these abstracts on a more concrete level, you can approach these swimming pool surface molecules from a diving board. To get the full theoretical impact, spread your body out flat as you leap. When you contact the water, the force you feel is, in large part, the extra work it takes to get those surface molecules out of the way.

Why a Bubble?

BUT WATER IS NOT the only ingredient you need in bubble-making. Water by itself makes lousy bubbles. For two reasons: One, water evaporates too quickly. The bubble wall is so thin, just a little evaporation pops it.

And two, bubbles are a lot of surface area for not much water. It takes work to make all that surface area. (Show me a bubble, and I'll show you a frustrated drip.) As a result, it's teetering at the top of an energy hill. And in the case of plain water, the hill is too steep. Water, in other words, is *too* sticky.

The missing ingredient, of course, is soap. Soap reduces the water's surface tension just enough to make a delicate balance possible.

An Experiment YOU Can Do at Home

Pour a little bit of water in a saucer and proceed to very carefully place a paper clip on its surface. If you do it gently enough, it'll float.

Now put a drop of soap into the water. The results? Sunken paper clip. The reason? Soap doesn't strengthen surface tension, it weakens it. Since surface tension makes possible large waves and so forth, you could, theoretically, pour soap over troubled waters as well as oil.

To understand how soap reduces water tension requires, once again, a short descent to the molecular level.

A molecule of soap is a long chain of carbon and hydrogen atoms. At one end of the chain is a collection of atoms that likes to be in the water. At the other is a collection that can't stand it. When mixed in the water, those soap molecules that find themselves near the surface wedge themselves between the water molecules and orient themselves with their "water-hating" ends out. As a result, the average distance between surface water molecules is increased, "weakening" the skin of surface tension.

Incidentally, it's this love/hate relationship to water that makes soap such a good cleansing agent. If a particle of grease is stuck to the surface of something, the "water-hating" ends of the soap molecules attach themselves so affectionately to the grease that they actually lift it off whatever surface it's stuck to.

One more small benefit. Since soap displaces water at the surface, it also tends to reduce the evaporation problem, thereby lengthening a bubble's life.

Why Does Less Surface Tension Help to Make Bubbles?

A BUBBLE IS JUST a drip's way of staying together when some force is trying to inflate it. Without soap to weaken the surface tension, the drip wins. Without some surface tension to hold things together, the force wins. When you drop a brick into pure water, the surface explosion produces a lot of droplets, but very few bubbles because water by itself won't stay put for all that bubble surface.

But when you drop a brick into a soapy solution, the water, in its weakened state, will get caught in a bubble formation and be unable to get back down to the lower energy droplet. The force that prevents it is air pressure. Note that this is a delicate balancing act, depending on *some* surface tension, but not too much. If a liquid (like pure alcohol) had too little surface tension, dropping a brick into it would yield nothing but millions of tiny droplets. There wouldn't be enough "glue" to hold the bubble together. Similar behavior to pure water, but for opposite reasons.

Water surface tension is not a heavyweight when lined up against most of the other forces it has to compete against. Gravity, a frequent opponent, almost always wins.

Take the case of Lake Superior, for example. There is a large amount of water in Lake Superior. But it is not in the shape that its surface tension would prefer, namely, a sphere, the smallest volume possible. The reason is gravity. It overwhelms surface tension effects and flattens the lake down.

RONALD BUCCHINO, a student of Harold Edgerton of MIT, took this remarkable series of photos of a drop landing in a saucerful of milk. The exposure was a state-of-the-art 75,000th of a second.

Note that, in spite of everything you've ever heard, drops are *not* shaped like drops. The sphere pictured in the first photo is the shape that a drop of liquid assumes in free fall where there are no other forces to deform it.

Many drops give birth to bubbles when they impact a liquid surface, but this one does not. The closest it gets is in the second frame when a "half-bubble" has formed. But before it can join at the top, it collapses. Not enough force to the impact to lift the liquid.

The water spout that forms, and then breaks, is an example of the attractive forces between water molecules. A "neck" in the water spout tends to collapse upon itself, breaking off the little sphere. This is precisely the same behavior evidenced when a long tubular bubble thins out into "necks" that oftentimes pop the bubble.

On the moon, the lake would still find it impossible to shape itself into a ball, since it would be held flat even by the moon's weak gravity. But surface tension effects would have more relative importance. Moon storms would be mountainous affairs, with a lot more airborne water as wavetops broke off and congealed together.

It would only be in deep space that Lake Superior could finally get loose of gravity and assume its "natural" surface tension defined shape— one huge drop.

On earth, the only time you can see surface tension winning out over gravity is in the very small scale, when the water mass is greatly reduced. Water beads on a window, for example, are a classic example of the David of surface tension holding out against the Goliath of gravity.

Why Divers Worry About Bubbles, Not Sharks

(and Why Whales Don't Worry About Either)

HERE IS A VERY uncomfortable parallel between carbonated soda pop and the blood inside a diver's veins when he is underwater. A parallel that gives experienced divers far more concern than Jaws.

Water is an extremely heavy material, as anyone who has ever had to carry a bucket of it can probably attest, and when you are under many feet of it the situation has some serious squashing potential. A basketball suddenly released into the deeps would instantly assume the shape and size of a pea, just as a normally inflated set of human lungs would, given similar circumstances.

The reason divers don't suffer this unpleasant fate has to do with the fact that their lungs are *not* normally inflated when they are underwater. Instead their lungs are inflated with high pressure air, taken at just the right pressure from their tanks to keep the weight of all that water at bay. It's a delicate balancing act that only works because of the accuracy of the feeder valves on their tanks.

However, the blood that carries all this high pressure air around to the cells quickly takes on the characteristic of bottled fizzy water. As long as the cap is on, the situation stays in equilibrium, but when the cap comes off (the diver starts to surface), the gas begins to come out of solution. The result can be very quick and very nasty as bubbles lodge in tiny vessels feeding blood to the brain.

The best cure is prevention. Divers are trained to surface slowly, exhaling continuously. In some cases, they will stop at certain depths for a specified period just to re-establish equilibrium. If a diver has surfaced too quickly, he has only two choices: get back down so as to force the bubbles back into solution, or get into a special chamber where the pressure can be adjusted as if he were back under water and surfacing slowly.

Incidentally, Robert Boyle, a 17th century scientist, accurately foretold this problem (called by divers "the bends") at least 100 years before anyone had the misfortune to confirm it. Other scientists originally dismissed the theory on the reasonable grounds that marine mammals, especially whales, seemed to operate quite happily in open defiance of it. It was known that whales fed on the ocean floor, thousands of feet below the surface. What happened to their lungs? Why didn't their blood bubble up when they surfaced?

A number of elaborate theories circulated for more than a hundred years as to how whales could swim serenely about at depths that would have miniaturized a set of human lungs. The answer turned out to be quite simple though: Whales don't take an inflated set of lungs to the bottom of the ocean. They exhale before they dive, they don't inhale. There's enough dissolved oxygen stored in their massive blood supply to fuel their cells for periods up to an hour and 15 minutes.

JOSEPH A. F. PLATEAU (1801–1883)
Although bubbles and soap film have attracted the interest of scientists through the ages (Newton did significant work in the area) it was Joseph A. F. Plateau, a Belgian physicist who died more than a hundred years ago, who's generally given credit for being the field's most important researcher.

Plateau made thousands of observations of soap bubble configurations in very tightly controlled experimental settings. It was he, for example, who first discovered that bubbles connect in only one of two ways. His findings, distilled over a lifetime of work, were published in a two-volume tract that still stands, more than a hundred years later, as the definitive work on surface tension effects in bubbles and films.

Probably the most remarkable aspect to Plateau's distinguished scientific career was the startling knowledge that most of it was accomplished despite the fact of his blindness.

At the age of 28, in the spirit of true 19th century scientific experimentalism, Plateau stared directly at the sun for a period of minutes to investigate an optical hypothesis he was testing. The result was a gradual loss of vision, becoming total more than 14 years later.

But the disability appears to have had no more than a minor effect on his productivity. He continued to devise novel experiments whose results he "saw" through the eyes of others, notably his wife, son and son-in-law. Indeed he did his most famous work during this period, adding an additional measure of renown to a career already assured a spot in the history of science.

The Colors of a Bubble's Lifetime

BLACK AND WHITE photos of bubbles unfortunately miss one of the primary bubble magicalities, their colors. A prism sprays a rainbow across a wall by virtue of the fact that light, as it passes through the prism, is spread apart into its various colors. (What we see as natural light, is really a blend of all the colors.)

But a bubble wall creates colors in a totally different way. As you'd remember if you'd paid attention in class, light often behaves like a wave which can bounce off a surface like the wall of a bubble. A ray of, say, blue light might bounce off the surface of the bubble wall nearest your eye, and off the surface of the wall furthest from your eye. Since one of these rays has to travel a tiny bit further to your eye than the other, their "waves" tend to interfere with one another. Sometimes the two waves might "add" together if their peaks synchronized. Other times, they might tend to cancel one another out if one wave's peak coincided with another wave's trough. The result is a shifting pattern of colors as light waves interfere with one another.

When a bubble wall becomes *extremely* thin, an interesting thing starts to happen. The wall of the bubble becomes thinner than the wavelength of any visible light. Without dragging you through the optical specifics, this results in a black appearing film. Light rays bounce off the surface of the bubble nearest your eye, and the surface of the bubble furthest. The two surfaces are so close, however, that the two reflected light waves interfere with one another and cancel each other out.

This thinning process starts at the top of a bubble since gravity "drains" a bubble just like it would a leaky bucket.

The practical result of all this gives you an ability to predict with dire accuracy when a bubble is about to breathe its last: look for the tell-tale black band near the top, the sign of impending doom.

Foams and Fizz

DUE TO A perceived lack of much industrial value, individual soap bubbles haven't aroused a great deal of well-funded research interest (a defect they share with such good company as snowflakes, spiderwebs, dewdrops, and other small acts of natural beauty).

The situation changes however, when masses of bubbles gang together creating foam. Practical utility rears its ugly head. Foam possesses uniquely valuable characteristics largely because there isn't much to it. It's mostly air, about 95%. But "packaged" in a unique way—held within bubble walls that are mostly water. The primary industrial uses for foam are in the application of things like dyes, chemicals, resins, pesticides and other liquids that need to be uniformly applied, often from a distance, and with a minimum impact.

The most glamorous industrial application is in fire and explosion control. Every urban fire fighting department in the country has foam generating equipment used in battling chemical fires and "contained" fires with limited access. The foam deprives the fire of oxygen while at the same time cooling it. Meanwhile, although less commonly, bomb squads occasionally use foams to smother suspected bombs. At the Sandia National Laboratories, nearly 100% of a bomb's force was absorbed by a thick layer of foam in a test explosion.

Here the San Francisco Fire Department trains in the use of high pressure foam to fill a burning airplane.

Dr. ARISTID V. GROSSE

Once The World's Leading Fizzicist
Dr. Aristid Grosse, for many years the director of the Research Institute at Temple University, spent his youth in the study of high-energy particle physics. He worked on the Manhattan Project, joined the faculty at Temple, became president of a well-known consulting company, published numerous scientific papers and, to all appearances, pursued a dignified, as well as distinguished, scientific career.

Meanwhile though, he was privately conducting a series of strange experiments that have made him an expert—probably the world's leading—on the subject of bizarre bubbles and funny foams.

Take "skyfoam" for example.

Dr. Grosse once modified a 55 gallon steel drum with a copper tube apparatus that looked suspiciously like a still. When connected to a tank of helium and a source of soapy water however, the drum suddenly began to spew out large gobs of aerodynamic foam. "Skyfoam," as it was inevitably dubbed, could climb to altitudes of 30,000 feet. As basketball-sized blobs of foam headed off into the blue, Dr. Grosse would speculate on the as-yet-unrealized practical applications to "skyfoam."

Speculation, incidentally, whether practical or not, was Dr. Grosse's strength. Once, after wondering about the ability of huge blobs of foam to quell street riots, he buried himself in a tankful of a specially formulated foam. "You can't see a thing," he reported back. "You can't hear a person three feet away unless he shouts."

Another application (which seems a tad more likely) would replace toxic pesticides with a special dense foam that would suffocate insects rather than poison them. Dr. Grosse believed the foam would be completely harmless to anything larger than a boll weevil.

Dr. Grosse used to experiment with special formulations of bubble solution that could generate gel-like bubbles with some very peculiar un-bubbly properties. For one thing, they could be decorated and hung around a room like party balloons. Dr. Grosse had several in his office with sequins on them (no less). He even had plans involving the creation of a 40 foot long hot-dog shaped gel-bubble that would function as a parade float.

Solving the Great Bubble Mystery

I T SHOULD COME as no surprise to anyone who has trouble getting up in the morning that the universe is most comfortable in its least energetic state. There are few laws of physics that crop up as frequently as this one; systems that *can* change, promptly do so in the direction of lowest energy. The sun, for example, is slowly burning out. Water, when given the thermal chance, freezes into ice. A desktop, to use an example close to my own heart, will, in accordance to these fundamental laws, slowly mound over with paper.

It was this principle that eventually afforded the key which enabled mathematicians to solve one of the longest running enigmas in physical geometry: Why do soap bubbles form in such regular ways?

The regularity of soap bubble shape has been an observed fact of nature for millenia, but it wasn't until 1873 when Plateau made the startling observation that bubbles could only join one another at one of two angles. A sinkful of suds might look a little disorganized, but each of the zillions of bubble intersections is either 109 or 120 degrees. There are no other possibilities.

This kind of bizarre precision in nature attracts mathematicians by the droves and efforts were made for years to work out equations that would explain "Plateau's problem." The search led to the creation of whole new areas of mathematics. In 1931, Jesse Douglas published a 60-page "solution" that was awarded the Fields Medal (the mathematicians' equivalent of a Nobel Prize). Unfortunately, it turned out to be only a partial solution that depended on a simplification of "bubble reality."

The basic forces that shape bubbles were already well-known: surface tension (the elasticity of the bubble skin) and the opposing air pressure in the bubble. Gravity plays a trivial role in bubble shape because of the tiny mass. (Bubbles in weightless space would look a lot like bubbles right here.)

Plateau's Problem was finally solved in 1975 by a team of mathematicians from Rutgers University. Their model appears to explain, in precise detail, the kinds of shapes that bubble film can form. The details of the proof are "horrendous" but the underlying principle that begins it is mathematically described as "area-minimizing." Roughly translated, the principle says that bubbles assume the smallest shape possible. In human terms, they cover the area that their surface tension forces them to, but they do it with the least amount of effort that they can. A comfortably familiar notion for most of us.

This "law of least effort" is not confined to bubbles. It operates on both the micro and macro scale and is discovered in some of the oddest places.

The scientist best known for his investigations into the "why" of natural shapes is the British naturalist D'Arcy Thompson whose book "On Growth and Form" is considered the classic on the subject. As Thompson makes clear, the same principles that govern "bubble clumps" also help determine the patchy coloration on a giraffe's hide, the organization of bee-hive cells, the way a dragonfly's wings grow, cracks in drying mud . . ."all systems—biological, physical, chemical—in which there is an economy of association of cellular shapes."

Randomness, which at first might seem to play a dominant role in the shaping of the natural world, actually plays a small part. Organization is the rule, not the exception.

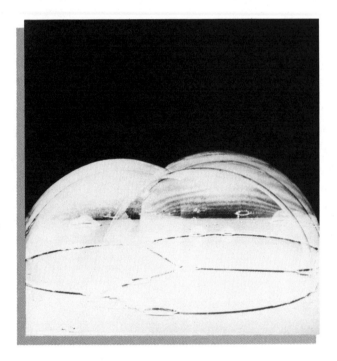

Permanent Bubbles

T HERE'S SOMETHING very un-bubbly about a bubble that won't burst, just as there would be something a little un-rosy about a rose that wouldn't fade. And if bubbles had the durability of footballs, they would probably lose a good bit of their fascination for us. Imagine trying to clear out a bubble-clogged sink with an ice-pick.

Fortunately, most bubbles rarely outstay their welcome. While Bubble Thing bred specimens lasting up to 4 minutes have been observed outdoors, they are the exception.

As it turns out though, bubble death is preventable, or certainly postponable, a discovery most definitively made by Dr. Grosse nearly 30 years ago. Among Dr. Grosse's many other scientific awards and achievements exists the lesser-known fact that he was once the owner of the world's oldest bubble.

Prof. Grosse's office was home to a huge collection of aging bubbles, in various stages of decay. Under Prof. Grosse's meticulous care, bubbles did not burst. They flattened. But it was a process that often took many months, in some cases, years. They were created out of an esoteric bubble solution, and protected from deadly dust particles by glass bell jars.

Prof. Grosse has described his peculiar collection in this way: "My first bubbles all died in infancy. They were blown with much the same kind of soap that Isaac Newton used in his classic bubble experiments. I turned to the literature and found that a much better soap was described more than a century ago by the blind Belgian physicist Joseph A. F. Plateau, who laid the foundations of our present knowledge of soap bubbles. Bubbles blown with Plateau's solution will last for several minutes in an ordinary room and for several hours with proper protection."

How to Turn a Bubble into a Well Behaved Household Pet

IN THE COURSE OF his experiments, Prof. Grosse established the principles of bubble health and long-life.

1. **Dust is the arch-enemy of bubbles.** Particles in the air cause more bubble deaths than all other causes put together.

2. **Carbon dioxide is a bubble poison.** And since we exhale carbon dioxide every time we breathe, blowing bubbles by mouth is a bit counter-productive. The warm moisture in breath also condenses on the bubble, diluting the solution and causing it to burst. For these reasons, breath-blown bubbles have the seeds of an early doom planted in them.

3. **Bubbles love cold.** Just putting an average bubble inside the refrigerator can extend its life five-fold. Putting one in an oven has the opposite effect. Prof. Grosse experimented in a laboratory freezer with bubbles blown from special formulas and managed to solidify them at the extremely low temperature of minus 120 degrees. What happens to bubbles blown with water and ordinary dish soap at very low temperatures still seems to be an area ripe for research.

Using just Joy detergent, a healthy dose of glycerine, and a little awareness of the points discussed above, you can make bubbles on a cookie sheet that last 10 to 15 minutes. The technique is as follows:

Put a little bit of Basic Bubbles with glycerine (5% or so) into the bottom of a cookie sheet and proceed to blow bubbles using a straw or small rubber tube dipped into the solution. The technique is to dip the straw in the solution, pull it out just above the surface leaving a little "window" of soap film on its end. Then inflate that "window" into a bubble that joins with the surface of the solution.

Since your breath contains carbon dioxide (bubble poison) it's preferable to use another source of air besides your lungs, i.e., a squeeze bulb, or squirt gun. If you don't have any such, don't blow your bubbles up with air that you've taken into your lungs.

When you have a decent looking litter of bubbles, you'll want to protect them from drafts and dust. Use something like a big jar that you can invert over the bubbles. You can tip the jar up just a little bit and put your straw or tube back underneath to blow enough bubbles to fill the entire jar. Leave the jar on the cookie sheet where the solution can keep the humidity high.

Now you have a bubblearium. Examine the inhabitants to check for color. You should see reds and yellows, signs of healthy bubbles. Unfortunately, their time here is rather limited and you will soon see the top bubbles developing patches of deadly black, evidence that the film at this point has thinned out to less than a millionth of an inch. From a bubble's point of view, not a good sign. (Roughly speaking, one minute in a standard soap bubble's life is the same as 45 human years.)

When you get into exotic formulas, far more impressive results are possible. The elixir of nearly eternal bubble youth is probably Dr. Grosse's "double-bubble solution" but it, as well as an excellent recipe described by Plateau, require laboratory conditions and experience. Both of them have created bubbles lasting more than a year.

There is, however, a recipe within reach of most amateurs that makes excellent bubbles capable of lasting a week or more, plenty of time to form a small emotional bond to a bubble. First described by C.V. Boys, the English experimenter, it requires three days and two medium-hard-to-find chemicals. See the bibliography for details.

Soda Pop Science

WO QUESTIONS dominate the field of beginner-level soda pop science. Are there any bubbles inside a can of soda pop before it's opened? And why does it go flat an hour or so afterwards?

The answer to the first is yes. Sort of. There are bubbles, but they are too small to see. They can't grow into a full-fledged fizz because of the fact that gas molecules are leaving them (owing to their high pressure) as fast as they are entering them. When the gas traffic goes back and forth like this at an equal rate, the liquid is at equilibrium.

As soon as the top is removed, the pressure on the bubbles is relieved and the gas traffic into the bubbles (and out of solution where they have "squeezed" into) becomes imbalanced. More gas flows into the bubbles than out.

The result? A $34 billion industry.

Later on, the gas flow stabilizes. There is still some gas in solution, but as it leaves it is once again replaced in equal measure from gas in the bubbles. If you were to suddenly take a flat can of soda pop to the top of Everest, it would get a whole new lease on life thanks to the effective drop in outside pressure, allowing more bubbles to form.

Jearl Walker, in his book *The Flying Circus of Physics*, recounts a cautionary tale in this connection.

Apparently a tunnel beneath the Thames River was being inaugurated in London sometime near the end of the last century. In honor of the occasion, and for the benefit of the officials and statesmen in attendance at the tunnel's bottommost point, a case of French champagne was brought along. Unfortunately, because of the aforementioned problems and the

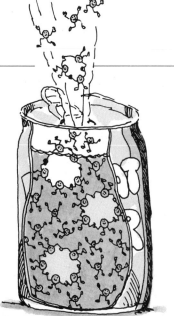

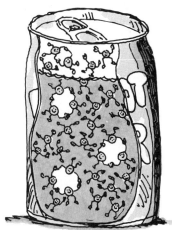

Root beer magnified 5 million times. Notice that in this can of unopened root beer, the density and activity of the gas molecules above the liquid is high enough to keep a lot of gas in solution. For every molecule that escapes solution, another hyperactive molecule re-enters it. It's a high pressure equilibrium.

Opened root beer, same magnification. Now the pressure over the liquid has been reduced. Not so many molecules are being forced back into solution. The traffic out of solution, into bubbles and off the surface, is higher than the reverse. The bubbles get bigger, rise to the surface and, frequently, spill all over the place.

pressurized atmosphere in the tunnel, the champagne turned out to be quite flat. Not to be discouraged apparently, were the celebrants, who proceeded to imbibe all of the champagne, bubbly or not.

When they returned to the surface (and a reduction in atmospheric pressure), the champagne began to abruptly revive. An observer afterwards described the scene thusly: ". . . the wine popped in their stomachs, distended their vests, and all but frothed from their ears." One dignitary had to be rushed back to the depths to undergo champagne decompression.

Such are the hazards of ignorance in soda pop science.

Bubbles, Boiling and Pasta

WHY DOES WATER BOIL? is one of those questions that only children are smart enough to ask. The rest of us are probably too scared—worried that the explanation will make us even dizzier than we already are. Actually, it's not too bad. And it has practical results, especially in the area of spaghetti noodles.

The bubbles that form in a boiling pot are actually filled with water vapor, not air as we normally think of it. Anything from porcelain to pancakes can be vaporized if heated enough and properly. Water vaporizes, at least in the presence of normal atmospheric pressure, at 212 degrees. At that temperature, the water begins changing into a gas and in fact cannot be heated beyond that point, no matter how high you turn up the stove.

Bubbles form at the bottom and sides of a pan during the simmer phase because of little irregularities that have trapped tiny bubbles of air. These little bubbles form seeds that the vaporized water can grow on. So much for theory. Now for the practical.

Every recipe that I've ever seen for pasta specifies that salt be put into the water before boiling. The standard explanation is that salt raises the boiling temperature of water, allowing the noodles to cook faster.

The only trouble is, it's a myth, at least at any reasonable concentration of salt. Try it. Take two pans of water. One with a couple of teaspoons of salt in it and one without. They'll both come to a boil within seconds of one another. If you put a *cup* of salt into the water, there might be some significant difference, but do you want to eat noodles cooked in sea water? My recommendation is to put the salt into the sauce for seasoning, or throw it over your right shoulder for luck. But skip the salt in the water, it's worthless.

R ICHARD FAVERTY is a well-known

Chicago photographer whose work appears regularly in national and international publications. Early on in his career, he received an assignment to shoot an incredible series of bubble photos for resale around the world, and, as he describes it, "I immersed myself in the job."

Twenty years later he still hasn't come out.

Now Richard Faverty describes himself modestly as "the human soap opera," a "bubble-ologist" extra-ordinaire and performing bubble person with television appearances around the world. Armed with a "secret bubble formula" and a unique set of bubble tools, Richard Faverty can put on a show-stopping display of bubble tricks, including the "bubble doughnut" pictured below.

By combining his abilities as a photographer with his bubble obsession, Mr. Faverty was also able to compile what must be the world's most impressive library of bubble photography, including a "surreal" series of photos of "bubbleized people."

Just another unique facet to a unique bubble person/photographer career.

Weird Bubbles

SOAP SOLUTIONS are far and away the easiest way to make bubbles and, as it turns out, also the best. Although it is possible to make bubble domes that adhere to a surface out of many kinds of viscous liquids (from syrup to tar), there are very few non-soap substances that can make airborne bubbles.

Except saponine. Saponine is present in, among other things, horse chestnuts. According to Charles Boys, an English physicist of the early 20th century, you can cut "horse chestnuts into thin slices and soak them in a very little water. The slightly yellow liquid contains enough saponine to enable platform bubbles up to 3 or 4 inches in diameter to be blown." The odd thing about saponine bubbles is their gel-like skin. When air is withdrawn from a saponine bubble, it doesn't burst, it collapses into "a wrinkled bag."

Gum Bubbles. Here we enter the world of competition bubbles. For the past few years, Susan Montgomery Williams of Fresno, California was reigning bubble gum champ. Then Vasnik Bains of London surged to the lead with an 11 inch effort accomplished in May 1986.

DR. ILAN CHABAY is probably one of the world's foremost authorities on the subject of frozen bubbles, having put together a frozen bubble exhibit for the San Francisco's Exploratorium bubble exhibit. Dr. Chabay uses dry ice in an enclosed box. The low temperatures freeze the bubbles and they float nicely on the carbon dioxide. The solution used, according to Dr. Chabay, is the standard soap and water.

Duplicating Dr. Chabay's bubbles on your own in the out of doors would take temperatures well below freezing and enough "hang" time to allow the film to freeze. A tricky set of conditions, but frozen bubbles *are* possible.

Dr. Ilan Chabay, Stanford University consultant, former associate director of the San Francisco Exploratorium, and frozen bubble magnate, demonstrates his "Frozen Bubble Box" exhibit.

How I Invented Bubble Thing

BY DAVID STEIN

The baby was 1½. I was carrying her around the corner when she spied a man relaxed against a green Chevrolet blowing dimestore bubbles with a little red wand. She sat up straighter in my arms, she was on the alert. She was staring. So we went down to the dimestore and got our own, and hunkered down right there on the corner and blew. This went on for months, bottle after bottle of bubble juice, she had to have it. Til one day we ran out, and tried dish soap and it worked. Which I never knew before. We were still doing it in August 1984 when we went to Maine for a few weeks, and in between tearing down walls to get the carpenter ants, and jacking up the cellar beams so the cookstove wouldn't fall through, and other ramshackle emergencies, we kept using dish soap. I started making little wire wands, tried a coffee can, a coat hanger, started thinking about a bicycle tire dunked in a little plastic swimming pool. And then I was lying in bed early one morning staring at the ceiling realizing this was an interesting design problem. To maximize the size of bubbles, you had to get the most juice up there in the right shape in a short time, and to do that you needed a huge loop, but such a loop should be collapsible so it could fit down into a small container. I then saw the first Bubble-what-ever-you-might-call-it in my mind, and when the hardware store opened I walked to town and bought a dowel, some steel chain, and some fastenings. You could open and close the chain loop with a washer riding on the dowel. I dunked this in a pail of thick soap mixture, the chain became a rope of solution, I opened it, and a film started to swell outwards. I got a tube. We were electrified. I got a sphere by accident and people started screaming. Then I realized you could shape the bubble by closing the loop. The neighbors were already screeched to a stop in their pickup trucks and walking up the lawn, and gigantic glistening spheres were sailing away over the treetops. Eight foot spheres. I was innocent, didn't know these were the biggest bubbles ever blown, didn't know I would sink my savings, spend two years patenting, testing, redesigning, building a business, I was just standing in Maine, a cold, beautiful thrill up my spine, neighbor kids running, popeyed, jaw dropped open, same as the baby staring at the first miracle bubble of her life, same as Bubble Thing crowds ever since, amazed, asking, "What's that bubble thing?" Which is why the name.

Postscript

JOHN P. HUCHRA is a faculty member of the Harvard-Smithsonian Center for Astrophysics and generally a very sober-minded scientist. He is also a co-author of a report on the largest mapping effort ever undertaken, a survey of the heavens that includes 1,100 galaxies. Galaxies are unimaginably huge star-clusters. Our own star is no more than an average member of the Milky Way galaxy, a smallish, backwater galaxy less than 100,000 light years wide.

After a great deal of computer-aided examination of the results of this survey, John Huchra and his co-authors began to see a kind of pattern emerge. It was not a pattern consistent with the existing "How-It-All-Began" theories—theories that put the force of gravity in the starring role. Rather it seemed to suggest that explosions were the primary shaping agents.

Dr. Huchra chose a rather down-home model to describe this pattern, which, if he and his co-workers are correct, would be nothing less than the shape of the universe, the grandest form of all, indeed The Pattern to End All Patterns.

"It's like suds filling the kitchen sink," Dr. Huchra says, "or maybe a bubble bath."

The surfaces of these universe-sized bubbles are formed by galaxy and super-galaxy clusters. Their interiors are pure voids, emptiness in its finest form.

A final confirmation of Dr. Huchra's cosmological bubble bath theory may be a good way off, but in the meantime, it has a comforting, star warming feel about it.

Bibliography

Books

Boys, C.V. *Soap Bubbles, Their Colors and the Forces Which Mold Them.* (1959 edition of an 1905 classic) Dover Press, New York. The most complete treatment in print. The language is a little quaint, and designed for budding scientists, but it is *the* sourcebook for all those wishing to delve deeper into soap bubble science.

Isenberg, Cyril. *The Science of Soap Films and Soap Bubbles.* Tieto Ltd. 5 Elton Road, Clevedon, Avon, England. A more modern discussion of soap bubble science, including a good bit of unadulterated mathematics. Quite thorough but not for the scientifically faint of brain. Available only from the publisher directly.

Preuss, Paul, editor. *Bubbles.* The Exploratorium, 1986. San Francisco. This is actually a special single-subject issue of a magazine published by the world famous Exploratorium in San Francisco with a number of articles written by experts on various bubble subjects. Informative and non-technical.

Zubrowski, Bernie. *Bubbles. A Children's Museum Activity Book.* Little Brown and Company, 1979. Boston. Written for kids by an experienced kid science educator connected with the Boston Children's Museum. Lots of home experiments. *Very* non-technical.

Articles

Almgren, Frederick J. and Taylor, Jean E. *The Geometry of Soap Films and Soap Bubbles.* Scientific American, July 1976. This is the "non-technical" explanation of the mathematical solution to "Plateau's Problem." Both Almgren and Taylor are mathematicians from Rutgers.

Grosse, A.V. *Soap Bubbles: Two Years Old and Sixty Centimeters in Diameter.* Science. August, 1966. A technical article on the "double-bubble" formula of Dr. Grosse's. Written for chemists.

Harvey, Frank. *Dr. Grosse and His Wonderful Bubble Machine.* Popular Science, November 1969. A non-technical discussion of A.V. Grosse and his bubble research and dreams.

Kuenhner, A.L. *Long-lived Soap Bubbles.* Journal of Chemical Education, vol. 35, no. 7, 1958. This is the recipe for Kuehner's formula. You'll need a laboratory and laboratory experience.

Steen, Lyn. *Solving the Great Bubble Mystery.* Science News. September 20, 1975. A journalistic, non-scientific report on the Taylor and Almgren bubble geometry work.

Strong, C.L. *The Amateur Scientist. How to blow soap bubbles that last for months and even years.* Scientific American, May 1969. A good discussion of A.V. Grosse and his amazing work with senior citizen bubbles.

Zubrowski, Bernie. *Memoirs of a Bubble Blower.* Technology Review. November/December 1982. Written for educators, by an educator, on how to use bubbles in a children's science curriculum.

Photo Credits

Credits

Special Thanks to:

Albie Weiss
Lindsay Kefauver
Mark Tuschmann
Anne Johnson
Alan Adler
Nan and Cody

Design, Art Direction and Production:
Stephen Rapley

Illustrations:
Sara Boore, Ed Taber

ISBN 0-932592-15-5

Book Printed in the United States
Bubble Thing manufactured in Taiwan

4   1   5   4

Free Catalogue!

Filled with the entire library of 100% Klutz
Certified books, as well as more Bubble
Things and a diverse collection of other
things we happen to like, The Klutz
Catalogue is, in all modesty, unlike any
other catalogue. It's free for the asking.

KLUTZ®

455 Portage Avenue
Palo Alto, CA 94306

(650) 424-0739

More Great Books from Klutz

Bubble Gum Science

Everywhere Backyard Bird Book

Chinese Jump Rope

Explorabook: A Kids' Science Museum in a Book

Face Painting

KidsGardening: A Kids' Guide to Messing Around in the Dirt

The Hacky Sack Book

Juggling for the Complete Klutz

The Klutz Book of Knots

The Official Koosh Book

Magnetic Magic

Shadow Games

Stop the Watch: A Book of Everyday, Ordinary, Anybody Olympics

The Klutz Yo-Yo Book